Chester

by ~~Mélanie Watt~~ Chester

DEAR Admirers,

Due to an OVERWHELMING amount of fan mail, I, Chester, am back with an amazing, brilliant, SMART, SUPER new book!

C.

To: Chester
From: Shakespeare
(Your #1 Fan)

CHESTER
n: Einstein

ester
PICASSO
(Your Biggest Fan)

Dear Readers,

Please forgive Chester. He's forgotten to mention that he wrote all those fan letters himself.

M.W.

For my sister,
Valérie ...who is much nicer than me.
But, more importantly, I would like
to thank CHESTER, the star
of this book, for being kind enough
to take time off from his busy
schedule to be in this sequel.
I OWE him BIG time!!!

First published in Canada by Kids Can Press Ltd in 2008

First published in Great Britain by HarperCollins Children's Books in 2009

10 9 8 7 6 5 4 3 2 1

ISBN-13: 978-0-00-727024-8

ISBN-10: 0-00-727024-0

Text and illustrations copyright © Melanie Watt 2008

HarperCollins Children's Books is a division of HarperCollins Publishers Ltd.

The author/illustrator asserts the moral right to be identified as the author/illustrator of the work.

A catalogue record for this title is available from the British Library.

Author photo by Tiness

Visit our website at www.harpercollins.co.uk

Printed and bound in Singapore

Chester's Back!

Chester

DO NOT DISTURB

Chester's BUTLER

Written and illustrated by Mélanie Watt's hero

HarperCollins *Children's Books*

A long time ago, in a faraway land, lived a cat named Chester.

I SAID...

A long time ago, in a faraway land, lived a cat named Chester.

NOT ready yet!

A long time ago ...

CHESTER, not THAT long ago!

BORING!

CAVE CAT take over!
Ooga Chugga Ooga Chugga!

A long, long, long, long, long, long time ago, in a faraway CAVE, lived CHESTER.

He was famous! He invented the WHEEL!

Little did the cave cat know that soon he would become extinct!

Now, Chester, let's try this again.

A long time ago, in a faraway land, lived a ... stinky dinosaur in need of a major breath mint!

Chester, get out from behind there!

Nope, THIS side looks WAY better!

CHESTER! CUT IT OUT!!!

Meet Mélanie, the bearded lady!
←

KABOOM!!!!!!

OPEN AUDITIONS
ON NEXT PAGE!

Mélanie Watt seeks replacement to play the role of CHESTER

Number 1, please step into the story.

Pffff!
Bunch of copycats!

OPEN
AUDITIONS

?

Line starts here

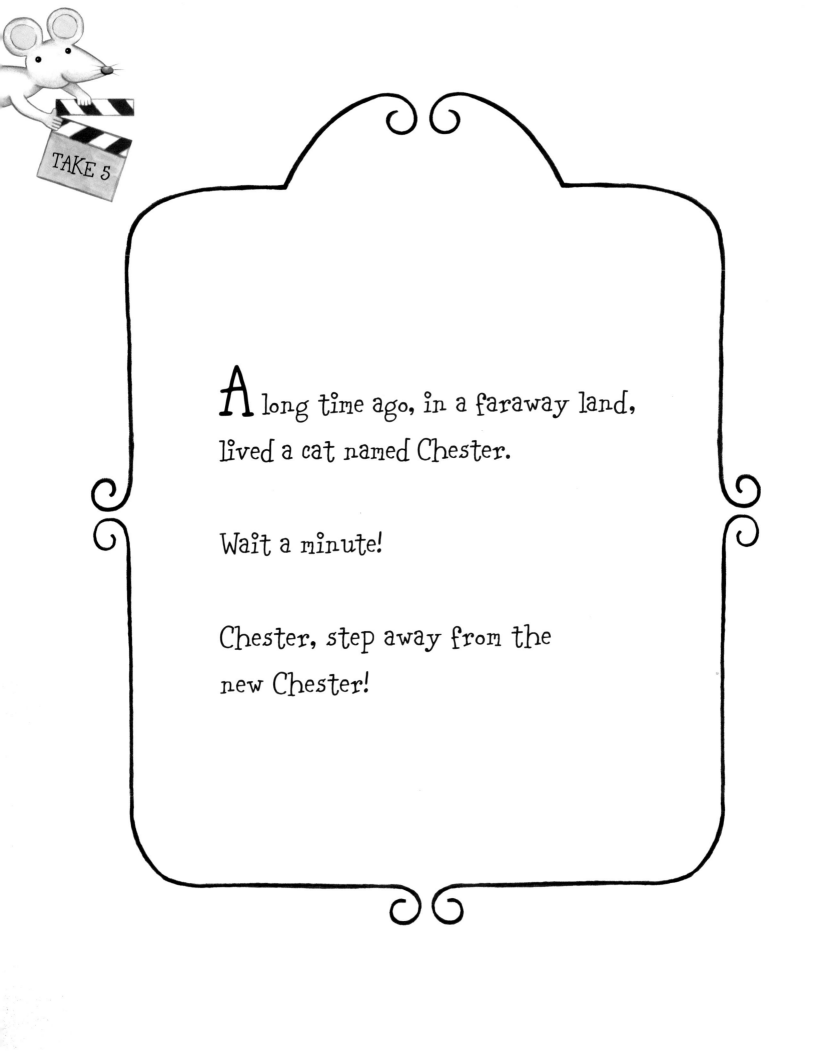

A long time ago, in a faraway land, lived a cat named Chester.

Wait a minute!

Chester, step away from the new Chester!

Chester, I give up!
WHAT DO YOU WANT???

GLAD YOU ASKED!
I want a story that
takes place in a LONG
limousine.

I want GIANT
billboards with
MY face on them
all over the CITY!

He's
unbelievable!

AND, since I'm VERY famous, I demand jelly beans but ONLY the red ones. AND... oh yes, my name written in lights! And when I arrive on the red carpet, I want everyone to see I'm a BIG STAR!!!

Is that it?

Mmm... and a bell so that I can ring for Mouse any time I need something.

Fine, Chester.

Hmm... make that SIR Chester.

Okay, SIR...
You asked for it!

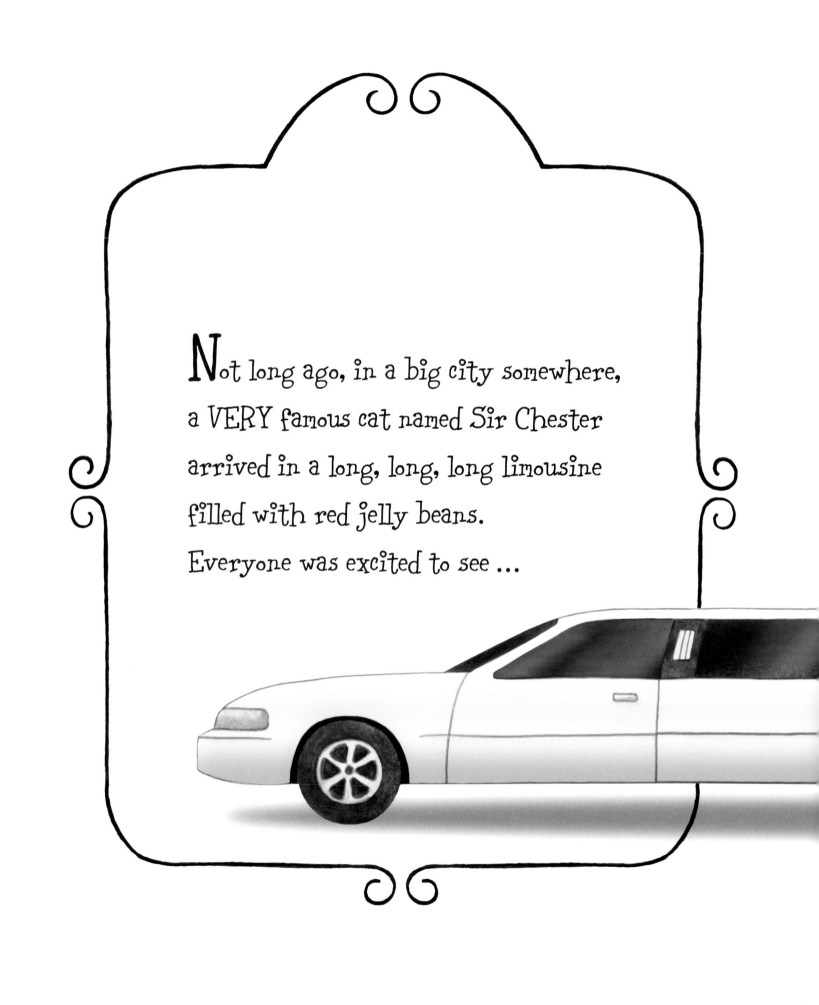

Not long ago, in a big city somewhere, a VERY famous cat named Sir Chester arrived in a long, long, long limousine filled with red jelly beans.

Everyone was excited to see …

...the BIG STAR!

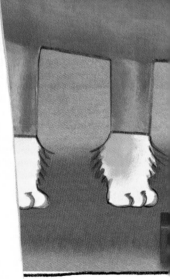

THE WORLDWIDE NEWS

SIR CHESTER TURNS HEADS IN FUNNY-LOOKING STAR OUTFIT

WHAT WAS THIS CAT THINKING?

That's NOT what I had in mind.

WANTED

Famous CAT seeks talented creator
to replace Mélanie Watt for next picture book!!!

REWARD

500 gazillion red jelly beans